W9-BXY-926

A DOG LIKE JACK

DyANNE DiSALVO-RyAN

Holiday House / New York

For Eddie, John, and Marja,

who helped me make a new family for Jack

Library of Congress Cataloging-in-Publication Data
DiSalvo-Ryan, DyAnne.
A dog like Jack / DyAnne DiSalvo-Ryan. —1st ed.
    p.   cm.
Summary: After a long life of chasing squirrels, licking ice cream cones,
and loving his adoptive family, an old dog comes to the end of his days.
ISBN 0-8234-1369-1 (reinforced)
[1. Dogs—Fiction.   2. Death—Fiction.   3. Grief—Fiction.
4. Pets—Fiction.]   1. Title.
PZ7.D6224Do   1999   [E]—DC21   97-41949   CIP   AC

Typography by Lynn Braswell

Jack was eight years old when our family adopted him from the animal shelter. That's fifty-six in dog years.

Jack used to live with another family before he lived with us. His other family had a fire in their house. They brought Jack to the animal shelter while they looked for a new place to live. But when they found their new apartment, no pets were allowed. I'll bet they felt bad about not taking Jack with them. I think his other family must have loved him very much. That's why Jack was so good.

Mom thinks that Jack must have come from a family with small children. Jack did not seem to mind when I wanted a pony ride. I would wear the cowboy hat my grandma gave me. Jack wore one of Dad's old scarves. Jack's paws made a noise on the kitchen floor that sounded like *chip, chop, chip, chop*. Jack and I grew up to be great friends.

When I started school, Mom and Jack would pick me up at three o'clock. Jack would wag his tail and bark a friendly hello to everyone. But even before Mom said, "Hi, Mike!" Jack would bark the biggest hello to me. On the way home, I would let Jack carry my lunch box. If Mom bought me an ice cream cone, I'd save the last licks for him.

On Halloween, Jack and I would go trick-or-treating. Once, I dressed up like a shepherd boy. Jack was a lamb. Mom cut a rectangle from a big piece of material. We pasted cotton balls all over it. I cut out two pink shapes for the ears, and Mom sewed them on top. We tied a bow under Jack's belly and one under his chin. Everyone laughed when they saw us. We got a lot of treats that year.

Each December, we would give Jack a red ribbon with jingle
bells to wear around his neck. I think Jack liked that. Mom
said it made a cheerful sound whenever he walked. She called
him Jingle Bell Jack.

Saturday was our special day to go to the park together. Jack would find squirrels to chase and bushes to hide in. I called Jack the Adventure Dog. When it was time to leave, Jack would jump over the park wall. He knew the way to go home.

But I think that Jack's favorite thing was to go to our summer house. The summer house was right near the beach. The beach sign said, "NO DOGS, PLEASE." So during the day, while I swam in the ocean, Jack would stay in his favorite spot under the shady pine tree. Jack was happy to be outside. At home in the city, we didn't have a backyard. So this was Jack's vacation, too.

At night, we'd take Jack to a beach that had no signs. Jack would run along the seashore. I would run after him. He'd get his paws all wet in the water. But my feet would stay dry on the sand. Jack liked the ocean. Dad called him an old sea dog. Every year when it came time for us to go back to the city, I thought Jack was always the one who looked the saddest.

In September, whenever my birthday came around, we'd celebrate Jack's birthday, too. On the day that I turned eight years old, Jack turned ninety-one.

We called Jack a good ol' boy now. On Saturdays sometimes, we'd still bring Jack to the park with us. He didn't run after the squirrels like he used to, so I would chase the squirrels for him. He'd wag his tail and watch me from the park wall.

On Halloween, when I dressed up like a monster from outerspace, I wanted Jack to come, too, but Dad said trick-or-treating would be too much walking for Jack. Jack sniffed me hard when I came home. He would have made a great alien dog.

When December came, Mom gave Jack his jingle-bell ribbon.
We didn't hear the bells jingle very much that year.

One afternoon I was playing in my room, when all of a sudden I heard a long, low howl. It sounded like Jack was crying. Mom and I ran to see what was wrong. Jack turned his head a little when he saw us. I bent down and put my arm right around him. Then Mom called Dad to come home.

Dad carried Jack down the stairs to take him to the animal clinic. Jack's back legs hurt him too much to walk now. The doctor listened to Jack's heart and checked his ears. "Take him home," the doctor said. "Give him lots of love and anything he wants." But Jack did not want anything. He just stayed in his spot by the door and hardly ever got up.

One day, when Mom went over to see how Jack was doing, she looked at him and began to cry. "Jack is not breathing," she said. Dad and I went over to look. I felt scared. I hugged Mom. Dad hugged us.

While Dad called the animal clinic, Mom and I went for a walk.

"Did Jack die?" I asked.

"Yes," Mom said. "Jack died."

"Do people live longer than dogs?" I asked.

"Yes," Mom said. "People live much longer."

I crunched my boot on the last bit of snow and watched the squirrels run like crazy. It was getting dark.

The next week, even though it wasn't summer, we packed the car to go to the summer house. It felt strange to be there without Jack. I felt like everything should look different now that Jack was gone. But everything looked the same.

We went to the beach and filled my pail with shells. When we came back to the house we all stood together under the shady pine tree. Dad dug a hole in Jack's favorite spot and placed the box of Jack's ashes gently inside. Then I made a circle of shells and pine cones. It looked really great.

Whenever I see a dog now, I always think of Jack. Sometimes it makes me laugh. Sometimes it makes me cry. Sometimes I wish I knew Jack's other family, just to let them know that we loved Jack, too.

I think someday we'll go to the animal shelter and adopt another dog. But not right now. Right now we still miss Jack. And to us, there will never be another dog like Jack.

Losing a Pet

How we find a pet or how a pet finds us is always a wonderful, loving story.

It's a good idea for families to decide together which kind of pet to get. Some families study picture books of dogs or cats from the library. Once a family decides what kind of pet to get, they might go to a shelter to rescue a pet or to a breeder.

When a pet comes to live with a family, a relationship develops, one full of joy, love, and fun. A pet often becomes like a person to us: a best friend, a sister, or a brother. We laugh with our pets, kiss and hug them, and talk and sing to them. We miss them when we are not home. Our pets make us feel good, and we enjoy lots of good times together.

As time goes on, our pets get older. They might become ill or have an accident, and, sadly, a pet might die. We might cry a lot, especially if the pet seemed like a "human person" and a family member. A family needs to know that it is all right to feel sad and cry, because the tears are "tears of love." They need to share grieving, because the pet meant something to each person. The family needs to talk together about the pet and share hugs and kisses as well as tears. Even teachers in school should be aware when children are going through this sad experience.

Children might have bad dreams, have trouble sleeping, find it hard to sit still, have trouble eating, or experience other problems. Other, surviving pets might have a hard time, too. They can miss their "buddy."

With time, we feel a little less sad, and start to remember our happy memories: how our pet made us laugh or how he could catch a ball. Remember the joy, love, and fun pets give us. They wouldn't want us to continue being sad.

To get over their sadness, children can keep busy, draw pictures of their pets, and talk to family members or friends. If there are surviving pets, they will need extra hugs and attention. If a family has any questions about a pet's illness and death, an appointment to talk to the veterinarian can help.

Children frequently ask about getting a new pet. It is a wonderful thing to do, but the family should decide as a group when they are ready for another pet.

MRS. KATHLEEN L. DUNN, M.S.W.
CHIEF SOCIAL WORKER AND COUNSELOR
THE VETERINARY HOSPITAL OF THE UNIVERSITY OF PENNSYLVANIA
PHILADELPHIA, PA